The Bad-Tempered Dragon

"Er, excuse me, but what are you?"

The something belched fire at them and said, "I'se a bad-tempered dragon, I is, and I'se come to stay, and youse as don't like it is going to look round one day and find yourselves all overdone and crispy round the edges. So there."

This was so exciting that two of the fishers fell over backwards into the river in astonishment, as the Bad-Tempered Dragon stomped up the quay and headed for the town.

More fantastic Young Hippo Magic stories!

Joan Lennon

The Bad-Tempered Dragon

Illustrated by Serena Feneziani

Hippo

For the Crumblies

Scholastic Children's Books,
Commonwealth House, 1-19 New Oxford Street,
London WC1A 1NU, UK
a division of Scholastic Ltd
London ~ New York ~ Toronto ~ Sydney ~ Auckland

Published in the UK by Scholastic Ltd, 1998

Text copyright © Joan Lennon, 1998
Illustrations copyright © Serena Feneziani, 1998

ISBN 0 590 19876 9

Printed by Cox & Wyman Ltd, Reading, Berks

2 4 6 8 10 9 7 5 3 1

Chapter 1

Black Cloaks and Woolly Jumpers

There once was a very junior wizard named Short and his companion who was a frog. Short was called Short because he wasn't very tall, and his companion was called Plantagenet because that was his name.

They went to Wizardry School.

Everyone knows that wizards are tall

and thin with great beaky noses. All the Senior Wizards who taught at the school looked like that, and most of the Junior Wizard pupils did too. Short, on the other hand, was small and weedy, and *his* nose had freckles and turned up a little at the end.

Wizards' companions are supposed to be sleek and superior-looking, like black cats or glossy ravens. They could often be quite bad-tempered as well, hissing or screeching at the drop of a pointy hat. But Plantagenet was bouncy and chatty and very, very green. And if *he* got mad, the worst anyone ever heard him say was a rather squeaky "Blarp".

Everyone knows that wizards always wear long black swirly cloaks while their companions sit up on their shoulders and look cross and proud. But Short wore warm woolly jumpers because you don't have to be much of a wizard to know that all frogs have very cold feet. And though companions usually have claws for holding on with, Plantagenet didn't, so that if Short stopped suddenly, *his* companion was likely to fall off.

When the class photo was taken, Short and Plantagenet were right there in the front row, looking short and woolly and green (at least, *Plantagenet* was looking green).

They were a strange pair.

The two went to Wizardry School in a large and prosperous town on the banks of the River Purpose. It was a fine town

with a shiny new supermarket full of special offers, a municipal fountain that was lit up by coloured lights in the evenings, and a Museum of Ancient Everything which nobody visited even though it was educational and good for you. Yet, in spite of all this, the town was not the sort of place to have stories told about it, because nothing exciting ever happened there. It was really rather dull. It was even called Dull – Dull-on-Purpose.

Dull was dull, until, out of the blue, something came to town that *was* worth telling a story about.

Chapter 2

"I'se Come to Stay!"

The something came sailing down the River Purpose on an empty, rather singed boat. The something was large and scaley and a sort of greeny-grey colour.

A few of the townspeople were fishing off the quay in a dull sort of way.

"What would you say that was?" asked one of them, looking upstream.

"Well ... it's a, sort of a, what you might call a ... boat. I think," someone answered.

"No, not the boat," said the first one. "It's the thing *on* the boat I can't quite place."

"Oh, the thing *on* the boat. Oh. Well. That's a ... at least I think it's a ... it's

bound to be a... Actually, I haven't a clue."

"Best ask it," someone suggested.

"Aye, it's sure to know," everyone agreed.

As the boat stopped sailing and bumped into the quay, the first fisher plucked up courage and called out,

"Er, excuse me, but what are you?"

The something belched fire at them and said, "I'se a bad-tempered dragon, I is, and I'se come to stay, and youse as don't like it is going to look round one day and find yourselves all overdone and crispy round the edges. So there."

This was so exciting that two of the fishers fell over backwards into the river in astonishment, as the Bad-Tempered Dragon stomped up the quay and headed for the town.

Wild rumours that something exciting was on its way spread all over town.

The Mayoress put on her best robe and chain and hurried out to welcome the dragon. The manager of Dull's shiny new supermarket straightened his tie, grabbed a handful of 2-for-1 coupons and raced to join her. The local branch of Mothers Against Everything was having morning coffee at Rosie's Café and turned out in force when the news reached them.

(They weren't Against Dragons at this point, but they *were* Against Missing Out on Anything.)

Soon everybody was trailing around after the Bad-Tempered Dragon, thinking How exciting! for at last something was really happening in Dull. But after a while, they started thinking How unpleasant! for the Bad-Tempered Dragon was appallingly badly-behaved.

Everyone knew that the Mayoress had been desperate to make a speech ever since she was elected thirty-six years ago, but nobody important ever came to Dull so she hadn't had a chance.

"Welcome to wonderful Dull," she said now in her plummiest Mayoress voice, as all the townspeople smiled proudly, "our lovely, large and prosperous town situated on the River—"

But that was as far as she got. The Bad-Tempered Dragon didn't listen. He didn't even try to look interested. Instead he gave a huge bored yawn, blowing black soot all over the Mayoress's glasses and setting her notes on fire.

"P... P... P..." spluttered the Mayoress, and the Bad-Tempered Dragon stomped on.

"Excuse me, excuse me," called the manager of the supermarket as he tried to catch up. "Could I interest you in our 2-for-1 Bonanza Extra-Special Special Offer?"

The Bad-Tempered Dragon stopped a moment and looked at the handful of Bonanza Extra-Special Special 2-for-1 coupons the manager was waving at him. Then he ate them.

The manager was so surprised he just stood there with his mouth open, as the Bad-Tempered Dragon stomped on up to his shiny new supermarket and through the automatic front doors.

Then the Bad-Tempered Dragon had a chew on everything in sight, including the Special Offer signs. He went joy-riding on all the supermarket trolleys, and bent their frames so that not only would they not go straight, they wouldn't go at all. He turned the Fresh Bread Department into the Burnt Toast Department, and the Frozen Food Department into the Defrosted and Then Some Department. And when a nice lady in a frilly apron politely offered him some little cubes of cheese on toothpicks, he didn't even say thank you, and he did melt the tray they were on.

The manager went home with a headache and the Bad-Tempered Dragon stomped on.

Dull had a beautiful municipal fountain in its fine Town Square which was lit up every evening with coloured lights. And by the time the Bad-Tempered Dragon had finished with that, two-thirds of the members of Mothers Against Everything had fainted, and the Secretary was already starting on her third sign Forbidding *Anyone* to Dabble their Fingers in Municipal Fountains Ever Again.

Then the Bad-Tempered Dragon was tired. He went to Dull's best hotel and made them bring all the duvets and all the pillows from all the bedrooms into the Grand Ballroom, which *he* said was the only place big enough for him to sleep in.

And when Dull's Golden Trotters Dancing Club (who had only just caught up with the crowd) very politely reminded him that tomorrow at 9.00 a.m. sharp they were meant to be learning the Samba, he made rude noises at them.

The townspeople looked at each other in horror.

"What shall we do?" someone asked.

They all scratched their heads and thought hard.

"Um..." said someone.

"Er..." said someone else.

"Well..." said someone else again.

"AhHA!" said the voice of a little old lady at the back of the crowd. "I've got it!"

Everyone turned to look. In fact the sight of all those townspeople staring at once made the idea (which had to do with knitting an enormous cage and putting the dragon *and* the Grand Ballroom in it and then somehow getting wheels underneath and rolling the whole lot into the river at midnight, and therefore *probably* wouldn't have worked anyway) go right out of her brain.

"Or ... or perhaps a *better* idea," quavered the little old lady, who was now blushing furiously, "would be to go and ask the Wizards."

The townspeople looked at each other again. Wizards, good for something? Then, as one, they headed for the School of Wizardry.

Chapter 3

The Attack of the Senior Wizards

Next morning, the most Senior Wizard called the entire school to assembly. She was extremely tall and incredibly thin and had a nose that would have made an eagle envious. She was not a Headteacher who had problems with discipline.

She stood at the front of the hall in her

black clothes for a long, dramatic moment. Then she said in a shivery voice,

"Ridding a Large and Prosperous Town of Bad-Tempered Dragons."

There was another long, dramatic pause. Then,

"Watch and learn!" said the most Senior Wizard as she swirled her black cloak and strode off.

The other Senior Wizards swirled *their* black cloaks and strode after her.

And all the Junior Wizards clattered up the stairs to the very top tower for a better view.

Dull's School of Wizardry looked out over the town from the top of a hill, and the top tower of the school was an excellent place for getting fresh air and keeping an eye on the neighbours at the same time. For a long while, however, everything seemed peaceful below. Then, "Look!" called one of the Junior Wizards.

A plume of smoke was moving above the streets that led from the River Purpose.

The Bad-Tempered Dragon was returning from his bath. The Junior Wizards could hear him humming, terribly out of tune, as he reached the Town Square and stretched out in the sun to dry.

Then the Junior Wizards began to nudge one another excitedly and point. Creeping up along one of the side streets, they could see the most Senior Wizard. And even from this distance, they could see that the jar she was holding was full of something very bubbly, very wizardly, and very purple.

Then Short nudged Plantagenet. On another side street was a sword and a disgruntled-looking raven, travelling along in mid-air without any visible means of support.

"Invisibility Spell Number 6," said Short.

"He forgot the last instruction," snorted Plantagenet.

"What's that?" asked Short.

"Thou shalt not pick anything up after ye spell is complete—"

"No, *that*! and what's *THAT*!" Short was pointing to another side street, and then another.

Converging on the Town Square, along the dozens of little streets, were dozens of Senior Wizards. They came clutching potions and powders, cloaks and ropes, dragon-proofed brooms and magical toothbrushes.

The Junior Wizards looked at each other in amazement. This was going to be worth watching.

There was a moment of absolute stillness, and then it began.

"KA-BLAMM!"

"Have at thee!"

"Take that, foul serpent!"

"One, two, out goes you!"

"By hook or by crook, I'll bop you with this book!"

"CRASH!"

"BANG!"

"Ooops!"

"Sorry..."

Purple smoke filled the Square, pierced by flashes of lightning and the odd stray firework. Soon the Junior Wizards couldn't see *what* was going on, though they could hear plenty of

thumping and coughing, and the sound of people falling over each other.

Then,

"RoarRRRR!" said the Bad-Tempered Dragon. "Youse is pestering me. When I is counted to five I want youse GONE. I'se counting now. One – six – three – FIVE!"

The Bad-Tempered Dragon was not good at counting, but it didn't seem to matter. As the purple smoke began to clear, they could see that there were *no* wizards left in the Town Square.

There was only the sound of sniggering, as the Bad-Tempered Dragon lay in the sun.

As the Junior Wizards came down from the top tower, they were strangely quiet. If the best efforts of the tallest and thinnest of the school's most Senior Wizards only succeeded in making the Bad-Tempered Dragon laugh, what hope did Dull have?

Chapter 4

"Don't Drop That Jar!"

The next morning, late, the whole school was called to assembly once more.

The most Senior Wizard stood at the front of the hall. Her black cloak was tattered, she had purple smudges in her hair, and her eyebrows had been singed off. The other Senior Wizards didn't look much better.

"Until further notice," said the most Senior Wizard in a tired voice, "everyone's assignment is as follows: 'Ridding ... ahem ... a Large and Prosperous Town of Bad-Tempered Dragons.' Anyone with questions will find us in the Senior Wizards' Staff-room."

The Senior Wizards limped off, and all the Junior Wizards raced for the labs to start their exciting new assignment.

Short tried to race too, but unfortunately Plantagenet wasn't ready and immediately fell over backwards. By the time they'd sorted themselves out and reached the labs, all the cauldrons

and most of the jars of purple stuff had already been spoken for. All around them there was a babble of spelling and mis-spelling as Junior Wizards settled to their work.

Plantagenet and Short looked at one another.

"Maybe there's something left at the back of the cupboards. You try that one, and I'll look here," said Short.

Plantagenet nodded and hopped off.

Wizard cupboards are well known for having strange and wonderful things overlooked at the back of them, but Short didn't have much luck with his. The dust that was getting in his hair and up his nose wasn't very strange, or wonderful either. He was sneezing so hard he had to come out of the cupboard and sit down.

Suddenly Plantagenet called. Short couldn't see him at first, but then there was the frog, backing out of another cupboard, clutching a jar. He called again,

"I'm here! Over here!"

He sounded really excited.

Something whispered *Trouble!* in Short's brain. Something whispered *Lunchtime!* in Short's stomach. This always happened when he was nervous.

"And bring some water with you!" called Plantagenet. Reluctantly Short did as he was told.

"Pour it into the jar," said the frog. Short tried to read the label at the same time, but it was so old and cobwebby he couldn't tell what it said.

"Now look deep into the jar," ordered Plantagenet, "and tell me what you see."

Short looked. He saw nothing but a sort of sludge. His heart sank.

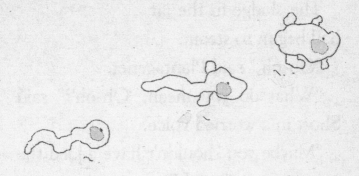

"Oh, Plantagenet," he groaned. "This isn't going to be like watching your home movies, is it? Not 'This is me as a tadpole', 'This is me just before I lost my tail', 'This is—'"

"Look deeper, Short!" interrupted Plantagenet. "This is no ordinary sludge. It isn't even the very special sludge from my own home pond. You are looking at Prehistoric Sludge!"

"Excuse me?" said Short, but Plantagenet's already bulging eyes were starting to pop out of his head.

The sludge in the jar
had begun to steam.

"Oh-oh," said Plantagenet.

"What do you mean, 'Oh-oh'?" said
Short in a worried voice.

"Maybe you shouldn't have added the
water just yet," said Plantagenet.

Short was starting to say, "But you told
me to!" when Plantagenet thrust the
steaming jar into his hands and hopped
up on to his shoulder.

"Let's go!" urged the
frog, holding on tight
to Short's ear.

They raced from the lab, scattering startled Junior Wizards as they went, and tumbled out into the street.

"But where are we going?" panted Short.

"To the Museum of Ancient Everything," was the answer, "and DON'T DROP THAT JAR!"

Chapter 5

Short Scales the Heights

Inside the Museum it was still and dim.
Plantagenet peered at the floor plan and
then hustled Short down a corridor to
the Great Hall.

"The Bad-Tempered Dragon!" gasped
Short, but it was only a huge skeleton. A
huge dinosaur skeleton.

The thing loomed over them out of

the shadows. Somehow the word "big" just didn't seem big enough.

"All right, Short, it's up to you now," whispered Plantagenet.

"What?!" squeaked Short, and back came a horrible squeaky echo from high up in the Great Hall. "*What?! What?!*"

"Somebody's got to get the Prehistoric Sludge into the dinosaur's mouth," insisted Plantagenet. "And you're the tallest somebody here."

Short stared at him.

"And could I just add," said the frog, "that you've very little time left. This sludge is due to go off in three minutes and forty-two seconds, exactly."

"Go off?" said Short. He was puzzled. "You mean it's going to go bad?"

"No," answered Plantagenet. "I mean, it's going to explode."

Short looked at the frog. He looked at the jar. He looked at the head of the skeleton, high above. All the things that had whispered *Trouble!* and *Lunchtime!* to him before had stopped whispering. Now they were shouting, *Get out! Get out!*

Short gulped.

"This is no time to get cold feet!" screeched Plantagenet.

"Look who's talking!" snapped Short, who was trying to think.

The frog was hopping up and down so fast he blurred. "Use a spell! Use a potion! Use an incantation!"

"Use a table," said Short, shortly.

"Oh," said Plantagenet, and he stopped hopping and came as close to blushing as anyone as green as that could. "Right. Good idea."

Huffing and puffing, Short pushed a table over from the wall to under the skeleton's head, and climbed up.

Not tall enough.

Puffing and panting, he heaved a chair on to the table, and climbed up.

Still not tall enough.

Knees shaking, Short up-ended a metal wastepaper bin, pushed it on to the table, piled it on to the chair, and climbed up.

It was just tall enough.

"You could hurt yourself messing about on a contraption like that," said Plantagenet, from a safe distance away on the floor.

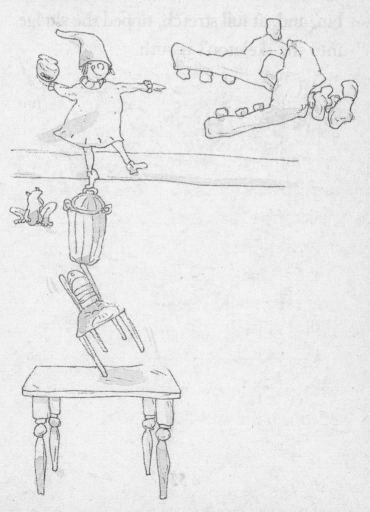

Short, who was holding a jar due to explode in fifteen and a half seconds, exactly, did not answer. He just gritted his teeth to stop them chattering, balanced as well as he could on top of the bin, and, at full stretch, tipped the sludge into the skeleton's mouth.

Then he fell off the bin, the chair, *and* the table.

For the skeleton had moved.

"That was delicious," it said. "Got any more?"

Short was on the floor trying to rub all his bumped bits, but Plantagenet boldly hopped forward and said, "Sorry, that's it."

"Too bad," said the skeleton regretfully. "Now, how can I help?"

Chapter 6

Cracking Down on the Egg

Outside in the sunlight, the Bad-Tempered Dragon had discovered Dull's children's playground. His eyes gleamed. He kicked all the sand out of the sand-pit, bent the climbing frames, and snapped the see-saw. He was just about to use the chains from the swings to floss his teeth, when he heard an unexpected sound.

Thud! Thud!

The Bad-Tempered Dragon turned a paler greeny-grey. The ground was trembling.

Thud! Thud!

Suddenly it stopped. The Bad-Tempered Dragon fearfully turned his head. His jaw dropped, then he shrieked and covered his face with his claws.

"*Well!*" said a disgusted voice. "That an egg of an egg of an egg of mine should behave like this!"

The Bad-Tempered Dragon looked about him at the wreckage, and burped an apologetic flame.

"Say excuse me. And cover your mouth."

"Yes, Greater-than-Great-Grandmama," whispered the Bad-Tempered Dragon.

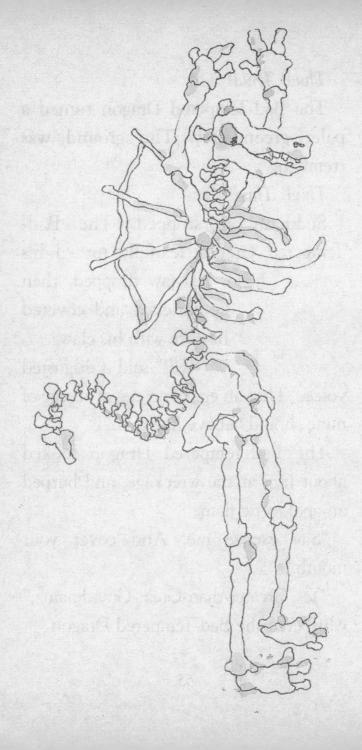

"And tidy this mess."

"Yes, Greater-than-Great-Grandmama."

"And the hotel and the supermarket, whatever they are. And make sure you CLEAN OUT THE FOUNTAIN!"

The Bad-Tempered Dragon hung his head, blushed a rather dingy brown, and said in a voice you could hardly hear,

"Yes, Greater-than-Great-Grandmama. Sorry."

"I should think so. Evolution has a lot to answer for, if you ask me. Oh, and give the Museum of Ancient Everything a dust while you're at it. Especially the Great Hall."

And the enormous skeleton looked down at Short and Plantagenet, standing carefully clear of her big feet, and smiled.

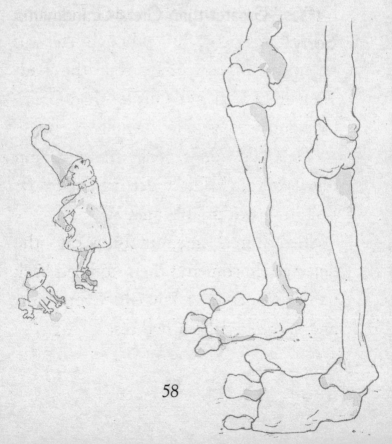

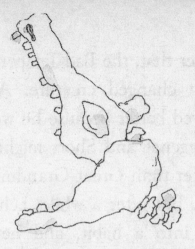

Then, all of a sudden, she opened her huge, boney mouth wide. For one horrible moment, Short thought she was about to swallow them, but the Bad-Tempered Dragon's Greater-than-Great-Grandmama was only yawning.

"Delicious sludge, that," she said, "but it's wearing off. I'll be getting back now. But any more trouble and…"

She glared meaningfully at the dejected dragon, and then stomped back to the Museum of Ancient Everything, and another well-earned rest.

After that, the Bad-Tempered Dragon was a changed creature. At first he behaved better because he was terrified Plantagenet and Short might bring his Greater-than-Great-Grandmama back again. But after a while, behaving well grew into a habit, and he gradually became known as the Well-Tempered Dragon.

He became very fond of the Museum of Ancient Everything and liked stomping about dusting things in it. He took particularly good care of the Great Hall.

Short and Plantagenet were heroes. Now when the class photo was taken, all the other Junior Wizards were wearing woolly jumpers, and all the other companions were trying to look bouncy and not using their claws to hold on.

The Mayoress ordered that a statue of Short climbing up to the dinosaur's mouth, with Plantagenet encouraging him, should be made. A famous modern sculptor came all the way from somewhere important to do it. The local

branch of Mothers Against Everything insisted that there be a sign nearby saying "Don't Try This at Home". But because the statue was so *very* modern, it wasn't clear what was happening, so there wasn't much danger.

Short and Plantagenet continued to make a wizard good team, even though the boy never did get much taller, and the frog never became less green.

And the townspeople of Dull were happy. For although their town was once again not the sort to have stories told about it, as a place to live in it was much more pleasant.

The End